I ~~Don't~~ Know How I Feel:

Helping young boys with

emotional intelligence

and fluency

Written by

Durdana Yousuf

Idea by

Rylan Ricchiuto

Illustrated by

Charity Russell

DEDICATION

This book is dedicated to all the young children who take the courage to become in touch with their feelings and allow themselves to express it in a positive way.

ACKNOWLEDGMENTS

I am grateful that Rylan Ricchiuto shared his feelings and his story. The stair of emotions on page 23, is inspired by Dr. David Hawkins' Map of Consciousness.

AUTHOR'S NOTE

The contrast between how boys and girls are brought up is very apparent when it comes to managing feelings. If a parent doesn't tell their young son to "man up" by suppressing his feelings, then a well-meaning teacher or someone else will do the job. The effects of this detrimental attitude lasts a life-time unless stopped and reversed.

It is my sincere hope that more parents and caretakers of young boys will make an intention and take action to allow the boys a chance to grow up in an emotionally healthy environment.

Something is weighing me down, but I don't know how to say it.

I don't know what I feel . . . or . . . how I feel.

Maybe I don't know how I feel, because if I know how I feel, I might want to share them with someone.

I don't like to share my feelings with others. They might think I am a baby and boys are supposed to be brave.

So I keep my face straight, even when my heart hurts, and tears want to come out and flow.

I hate it when my lips quiver when I am on the verge of crying.

Most of the times I am able to swallow my feelings and get my face straight. But that makes me feel more sad and heavy inside.

Sometimes, if my mom sees me like this she gives me a hug; she wraps her arms around my shoulders and squeezes me to her heart. That does make me feel a little better.

Just a little.

The feelings still fight inside me to come out as tears.

Hugs are nice; they are a symbol of love and acceptance. I like being loved and accepted by my family, especially my mom.

She says to channel my feelings as words through my mouth so I do not have to channel ALL of them as tears through my eyes, but it is ok if I do shed tears. She also gave me an option to channel feelings as written words in a journal.

She pointed out that I am exhibiting Ostrich behavior. When there is danger, an Ostrich has a habit of burying its head in sand, hoping the problem will go away and solve itself.

I guess I need to solve this challenge myself and not be an Ostrich.

To tell you the truth, I wish I could tell what I am feeling. It would be nice if I could tell the difference between feeling hurt, angry, or sad and how much.

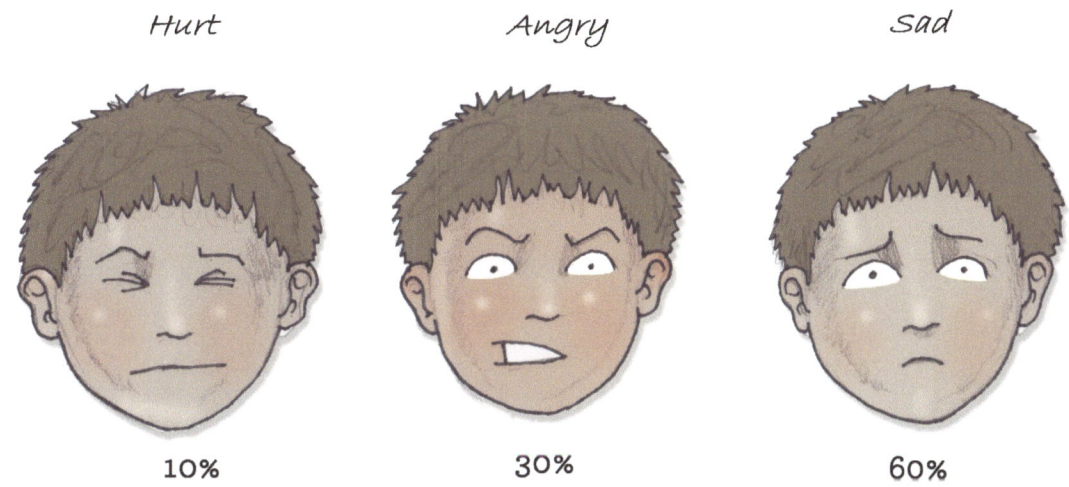

Hurt	Angry	Sad
10%	30%	60%

Like, am I more angry than sad?

And which feeling came first?

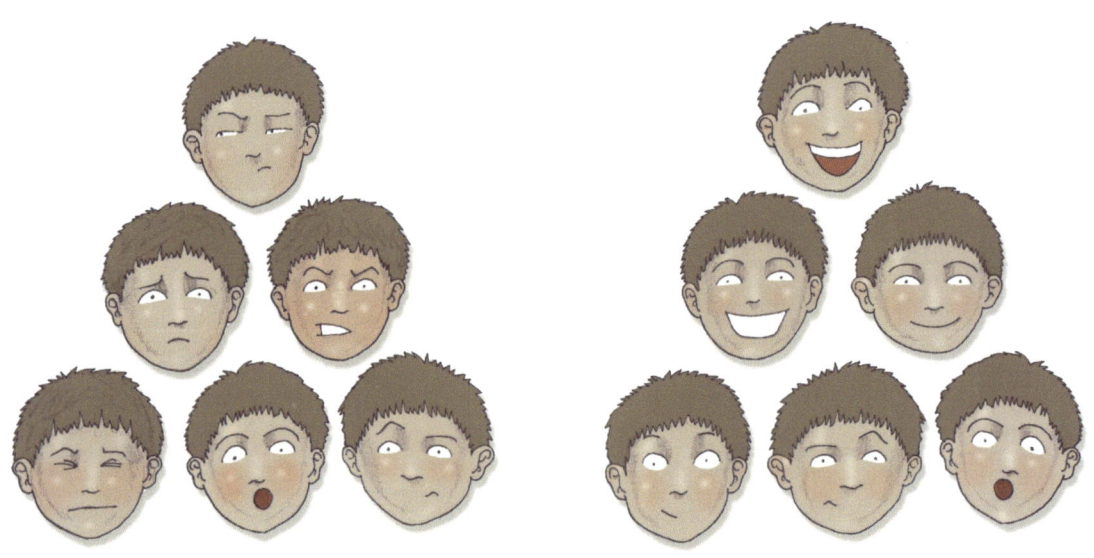

And not just these negative feelings. I wish I could feel the positives ones as well. Like joy, happiness, excitement, even neutral ones like suspense and curiosity . . .

When I think about my feelings, they feel like a messy jumble that I cannot identify. Like stars at night; so many that I don't know the names of. Sometimes, my feelings look like twisted yarn threads, waiting to be unraveled and wrapped again in a neat ball.

Maybe identifying feelings is like solving a jigsaw puzzle. Maybe I can identify one emotion . . . then the next . . . then another, until they fit like a puzzle, and that can tell me how I feel!

Let me try and see if I can identify JUST ONE of my feelings. Hmm . . .

I think . . . I was feeling sad.

But I think I was feeling more than just sadness.

I might have been a little angry too. And maybe resentful?

Why am I feeling, sad, angry and resentful . . .

. . . all at the same time?

Well . . . I think I know why.

Because . . . because, Ian won't let me sit next to Nate on the school bus!

That made me very sad. It made me so sad, that all I could imagine was . . .

. . . getting sick.

(The boy takes a

deep breath

and his

mood lightens up

a little.

A new thought

come to his mind.)

I wonder what happens if you mix feelings up? Are they like colors?

I wonder if feelings are like a rainbow? Do they change into another word if they are more intense? Do they change into another emotion if mixed with another emotion?

Do they start out simple and then become another feeling? If two feelings are combined do they create a different feeling like mixing colors make a new color? I wonder what emotion will emerge if a sad emotion was mixed with an angry emotion?

Or an angry emotion mixed with hate?

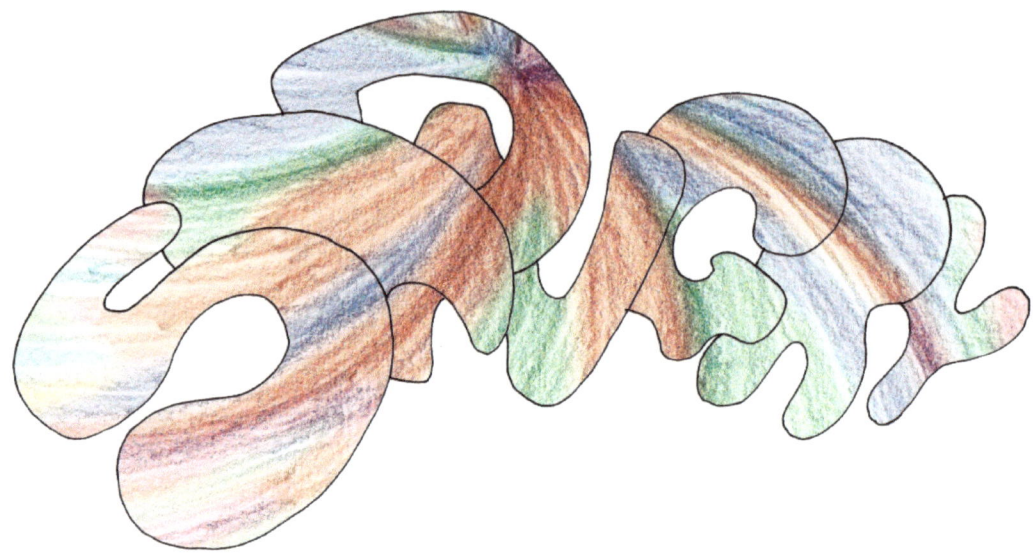

What will become of joy, if mixed with hope?

Hope mixed with gratitude?

I love being thankful and I have a bowl full of colorful crystals to create a "gratitude train" as a way for me to count my blessings!

Gratitude mixed with ecstasy? I get ecstatic when my mom lets me have a new video game or have a picnic in the park while watching 4th of July celebrations!

Now what steps can I take to get myself out of the negative and into the positive feelings?

Aha! Steps! Maybe I can climb my way out of them!

Yesterday, I got in trouble with the teacher for flipping mulch with a spoon and rolling pencils on the ground. She wrote that as a report to send home. I wanted to hide that report but my mom found it in my book bag. My mom asked me if I did that because I was bored.

I said, "Yes, and . . . I have no friends who would play with me." Again the tears threatened to burst out and I had to blink my eyes really fast so that the tears would dry up quickly and I tried to steady my lips as they wanted to pout and show hurt feelings. My mom hugged me and said, "good job explaining what made you feel sad. Being in touch with your feelings will help you have empathy for others' feelings as well AND have better friendships. "

I am glad that my mom didn't get mad about that report and that she allowed me to tell the truth.

I am also glad that I opened up to myself and met my feelings.

I feel much better now that I know what I am feeling.

I think, if we didn't have feelings, the world will be like those old black and white TV shows.

I like ALL of my feelings, even the sad ones.

Because, they tell me how I feel.